David Copperfield

Adapted by
Mary Sebag-Montefiore

Illustrated by Barry Ablett

Reading consultant: Alison Kelly
Roehampton University

Contents

Chapter 1
I am born   3

Chapter 2
Change   11

Chapter 3
I fall into disgrace   19

Chapter 4
School jungle   25

Chapter 5
A memorable birthday   32

Chapter 6
Aunt Betsey   40

Chapter 7
Ten years later   50

Chapter 1

I am born

My story begins before I was born. It was a bright, windy, March afternoon and my mother, Clara Copperfield, was sitting by the fire, her face flushed from sobbing. "To think," she said to Peggotty, her maid, "that my poor baby will be born fatherless. And maybe motherless too. Who knows if I will survive the birth?"

"Nonsense," said Peggotty, handing my mother a steaming cup of tea. "Now don't you fret, Mrs. Copperfield. You have me to look after you."

My mother looked up with a slight smile, but then let out a yelp of surprise and hid behind her chair.

"What is it?" cried Peggotty.

My mother could only point. A fierce old lady had her nose pressed flat against the window. "Oh!" she said. "It must be Miss Betsey Trotwood. My husband's aunt. I recognize her from her picture."

The next moment, Miss Betsey strode through the door and looked slowly around the room. "Mrs. David Copperfield, I think?" she said at last, taking in my mother's mourning clothes.

"Yes," said my mother, faintly.

"Take off your cap, child," Miss Trotwood went on, "so I can see you."

My mother obediently removed her cap so that her golden curls came tumbling out.

"Tut, tut, tut," said Miss Trotwood. "You're nothing but a baby, and soon to have a babe of your own."

My mother hung her head and sobbed, as if her youth were all her fault.

"Don't cry, silly girl. Listen. Your baby will be a girl. Call her Betsey Trotwood after me and I'll be her godmother and best friend."

"But... what if it's not a..."

"Don't contradict," said Miss Trotwood. "I have a hunch, and they're always right."

Before midnight that night, Peggotty was running for the doctor. "Clara's time has come!" she told him. "Hurry!"

Miss Trotwood waited downstairs, pacing the floor. "How is she?" she demanded of the doctor, as soon as the new baby's cry wailed through the house.

"Mrs. Copperfield is well," replied the doctor.

"No, she…SHE, the baby!" barked Miss Trotwood impatiently.

"Madam, the baby is a boy," the doctor returned.

Miss Trotwood instantly walked out of the house and never came back.

That baby was me: David Copperfield. We – my mother, Peggotty and I – lived in our snug little cottage, which had a garden brimming with flowers and butterflies. Our fruit bushes had berries bigger and riper than any I've seen since; our apples, firm, red and round, were just like Peggotty's rosy, smiling cheeks.

In winter we sat in the sitting room, where a blazing log fire lit up my mother's prettiness as I read aloud my books to her. I loved my crocodile book most, with its terrifying pictures. My home, in contrast, was utterly safe.

When I was eight, a man named
Mr. Murdstone began to visit our house.
He had dark hair and strange eyes,
so blank that you couldn't guess his
thoughts. I saw how his attention made
my mother smile.

At first he flattered me. "Come for a
walk – just us, David," he invited.

We went to a hotel where his friends
were staying: loud-voiced men, smoking
cigars whose fumes made a stale stench
in the room. They sprawled in armchairs,
surrounded by half-empty bottles of wine.

"A toast for Mr. Murdstone!" they
cried, pouring me a glass. "Drink to
'Success with the bewitching little
widow!'"

"What does that mean?" I asked,
sipping the wine.

They roared with laughter.

"Another toast!" they spluttered.
"Propose it, David. Say: 'Confusion to
young Mr. Copperfield.'"

"What do you mean?" I asked.

They found this even funnier. I knew they were laughing at me, but I was too young to understand why.

I saw Mr. Murdstone was at the root of it. Silent among his friends, I thought he looked evil. I wished my mother didn't like him.

"He'll leave us soon," I comforted myself. "Then Mother, Peggotty and I will be by ourselves again, snug and happy."

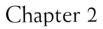

Chapter 2

Change

"Davy!" my mother said one day. "You and Peggotty are going to the seaside for a month, to visit her family. They live at Yarmouth."

"Lovely!" I jumped up and down excitedly. I'd never seen the sea.

Peggotty and I journeyed for miles by stagecoach.

"You'll love it in Yarmouth, Davy," she said. "You'll meet my brother, Daniel, and my nephew Ham. And there's his cousin, little Emily, same age as you."

The stagecoach stopped in a fishy smelling street and from there we walked to the beach.

"There's our house!" exclaimed Peggotty, wreathed in smiles.

I saw a black barge high and dry off the ground with a funnel sticking out of it for a chimney, smoking cheerfully. "That's not it?" I said. "That ship-looking thing?"

"That's it, Davy," said Peggotty.

She opened a little door cut into the side of the barge. Inside it was half ship, half house, and therein lay its magic. It had porthole windows, tiny furniture, and such a strong fish smell I felt I was being hugged by a lobster.

"I'm a fisherman," explained Peggotty's brother, Daniel. "'Course it smells of fish. Nice and fresh."

"C'mon, Davy," said Ham, kindly, as I hung back. "Let's go down to the beach." Off we trekked and little Emily came too. She was the prettiest girl I'd ever seen. We climbed the breakwater as the tide came in.

"Where's your mother?" I asked Emily.

"She's dead," Emily replied mournfully.

"My father's dead too. We're the same," I replied.

"No…" Emily disagreed, dancing dangerously on the narrow ledge above the roaring sea.

"I'm a fisherman's daughter, and you're a young gentleman. I want to be a fine lady," she added. "You have a much better time."

We played every day until the month was up. Going back home I was quiet, thinking of the seaside and the fun I'd had. I felt a little lonely; I wanted my mother and planned to rush into her arms.

Peggotty was unusually silent too, pressing her lips tight shut until she had her hand on our front door knob, ready to open it.

"I didn't like to tell you before, Davy," she confessed, "but you have a new Pa."

I shivered, guessing immediately it was Mr. Murdstone.

"Run in and say hello," Peggotty urged.

I did so, quaking with every step. On one side of the fire my mother sat sewing; on the other was Mr. Murdstone. My mother rose and opened her arms wide.

"Don't pamper him, Clara," said Mr. Murdstone. "Control yourself."

Instantly my mother sat down and went on sewing.

I felt as though an earthquake had ripped the ground from my feet. She loved Mr. Murdstone more than me! Nothing would ever be the same again.

I dashed upstairs and flung myself on my bed. Violent footsteps thumped up the stairs after me.

"You've upset your mother," hissed Mr. Murdstone as he flung open my door. "Bad boy! If I have a bad horse or dog, what do you think I do?"

"I don't know," I whispered.

"I thrash him. I say to myself, 'I'll conquer that animal if it costs him all the blood he has.' Now come downstairs to supper."

I obeyed. He was so threatening
that I was really scared. Yet if he'd said
one word of comfort, or welcome, or
reassurance that home was still home, I
would have tried to like him.

I wondered why my mother didn't
defend me. I understood, later. Now they
were married, she understood his true
nature. She was afraid of him. Very afraid.

Chapter 3

I fall into disgrace

I'd never been to school. My mother gave me lessons at home, and I learned quickly and easily – until now.

"I'll teach David," Mr. Murdstone said. "It's time he had some discipline."

Under his glare, I forgot everything I knew... words swam before my eyes.

After a few weeks, he banged his fist on the table.

"You are STUPID!" he yelled.

"I'm not!" I contradicted defiantly.

"Then you're lazy and obstinate." He swished his cane to and fro. "You must be more careful today," he announced. "I'm going to test you on mental arithmetic."

I was so mesmerized by that swinging cane, I answered every question wrong.

Now he was binding the end of the cane with wire. "He must be beaten," snarled Mr. Murdstone. "I was beaten myself as a boy, and it did me no harm."

"Did it do you any good?" faltered my mother, bravely.

"How dare you, Clara!" he thundered.

My mother ran up to him, clinging onto his arm.

"You're a fool, Clara!" he said.

My mother covered her ears and I heard her crying. Then, holding his cane, Mr. Murdstone pulled me up to my room, and twisted my head under his arm.

"Please don't beat me!" I implored. "I can't learn with you. I just can't!"

"Really?" he mocked.

THWACK! He swiped me hard. In response I caught his hand between my teeth and bit it as hard as I could.

He flogged me furiously. I yelled and shrieked and so did he. My mother and Peggotty raced upstairs. He pushed them away and locked the door behind him, leaving me lying on the floor, filled with pain and anger.

I was a prisoner for five days. On
the last night I woke to hear Peggotty
whispering my name through the keyhole.

"Davy! They're sending you away to
school tomorrow."

"School!" I was startled. "W-where?"

"Far away. Near London. Don't worry;
you'll be happier away from him. I haven't
come before because he wouldn't let me.
But I've never stopped thinking about
you. I'll hide a cake for you in the cart for
the journey. Look under the door, now."

She pushed through some coins. Then she kissed the keyhole on her side of the door since she couldn't kiss me, and I, kneeling, kissed the keyhole my side too.

The feeling I had for Peggotty is hard to explain. She didn't replace my mother; no one could do that, but I felt a love for her that I've never had for anyone else.

The next day I said goodbye to my mother. She looked pale and miserable. "You disappoint me, Davy," she said, coldly. "You must control your temper."

Mr. Murdstone had persuaded her that I was bad, and she believed him. That, to me, was his worst crime.

Chapter 4

School jungle

I climbed into the cart beside Mr. Barkis, the carrier man who was to drive me to school. Homesickness swept over me, and Mr. Barkis spread my tear-sodden hankie over his horse's back to dry.

"Hungry?" asked Mr. Barkis, eventually. "Peggotty, she said her name was – put in a cake for you."

"Yes!" I exclaimed eagerly. We shared it; Mr. Barkis was much struck by its taste.

"Never had such a good cake. What's her other cooking like? Pies? Pastry?..."

"Delicious."

He grunted thoughtfully. "Married, is she?...Or in love?"

"I don't think so."

"Well then, I'll drop her the word. Barkis is willing."

"You mean – you want to marry her?" I asked.

"That's right. If she wants to leave her job, Barkis is willing."

"I hope you'll be happy," I said politely. Privately, I prayed that Peggotty would never leave my mother alone with cruel Mr. Murdstone.

Two days later, we finally arrived. I said goodbye to Mr. Barkis who seemed like my last friend and met Mr. Creakle, the headmaster. His face was not reassuring – fiery red and bulging with purple veins.

"Here's your classroom, Copperfield," boomed Mr. Creakle. It was a long room bristling with rows of inky desks. It smelled like rotten apples mixed with mildewed books. On my own desk was a piece of paper, inscribed:

Beware. He bites.

"Where's the dog, Sir?" I asked, looking around.

"No dog, Copperfield," he said, tying the notice to my back. "Only yourself."

"Oh, Sir," I begged, appalled. "Please don't. The other boys will tease me…"

"Your stepfather ordered it," Mr. Creakle said. "I am a determined man, Copperfield. You will wear that notice."

Then he left me. I shrank against the wall, hiding my back, as the entire class swarmed in.

"Turn around, new boy," they chanted, twisting me in circles. "Show us what's on your back." It was like a nightmare.

"Stop!" ordered one boy, tall and handsome, with a friendly, easy manner. He was obviously popular because the other boys obeyed at once.

"I'm Steerforth," he said to me. "I hear you bit your stepfather."

I nodded. He looked me over and I looked up at him. "I expect he deserved it," he said at last, with a smile. Steerforth had saved me from the bullies. From that moment on, he was my hero.

"Got any money?" he asked.

"Seven shillings."

"Would you like a midnight feast? Do you like biscuits? Nuts?"

"Yes!" I said.

"Currant wine? Almond cake?"

"I like it all!" I replied.

"You shall have it," Steerforth said, kindly. "Just hand over the money."

That night, in the dormitory, Steerforth laid a sumptuous feast on my bed. "There you are! I'll share it with the other boys."

He did so, very fairly. Thus my popularity was ensured, but Peggotty's gift was all gone.

When I went home for the holidays, my mother held out a new baby.

"This is your brother, Davy. He looks just like you," she smiled, putting the white bundle in my arms.

"How dare you compare my son with yours?" Mr. Murdstone sneered. "Now, remember what you have to tell David."

My mother looked at me, her face pinched and white. "You can't stay with us here, Davy," she whispered. "You're to go to Yarmouth with Peggotty, until your term starts."

Peggotty and I left with some relief. My mother stood by the door, holding her baby, waving. That is how I think of her still, looking at me intently, and saying goodbye.

Chapter 5

A memorable birthday

Next term I had my ninth birthday. I was hoping for a letter from home, so I wasn't surprised when Mr. Creakle called me into his study.

"A visitor, Copperfield," he announced. I instantly thought my mother or Peggotty had come to see me...

It was Mr. Murdstone, his black eyes more inscrutable than ever.

"Your mother has died," he announced abruptly.

I was too stunned to think. Dead! I told myself, trying to take it in. Dead...

"The baby...?" I stammered.

"Fading fast," he said coldly. "Not expected to last the week. I'm not responsible for you now, though. I've come to tell you that you must leave school and earn your living."

"I can't do much," I gulped.

"Sulky as ever," he jeered. "I've found you a job in a factory, in London. Think yourself lucky. You'll live with a friend of a friend, Mr. Micawber, and pay him rent. Here's the address. Get packed and go."

"W-where's P-Peggotty…?" I asked.

"Dismissed," he snapped, and was gone.

In a haze of misery, I went to get my things. I had to do as he said, because there was no choice.

I had no money and no home. I wasn't even going to have an education. I knew that without it, Mr. Murdstone robbed me of my chance to make something of my life. I was driven to London, to Mr. Micawber's address, a house in a run-down backstreet.

A woman, clasping a screaming twin – the other was yelling on the floor – opened the door.

"Come in!" she whispered. "Quick. Don't let the debt collector see you. He's always skulking about, waiting for a chance to get in. Not that there's money here, or anything else."

Slipping inside, I saw the sitting-room had no furniture at all.

"I'm Mrs. Micawber," she introduced herself. "You and your rent are welcome! Poor Mr. Micawber has been very unfortunate in his finances. But I'll never desert him. Never! The father of my twins, the husband of my heart."

Mr. Micawber now appeared, in floods of tears. "My angel," he sobbed. "Thank you."

I stared around the empty room.

"Yes, everything's gone," Mrs. Micawber confided. "Even my pearl necklace and my bracelets, all sold to pay our debts. But Mr. Micawber is a man of great talent. He just needs a chance."

"I'll give you some advice," said Mr. Micawber. "If only I'd taken it myself! Income twenty pounds, expenditure nineteen pounds: result happiness. Income twenty pounds, expenditure twenty one pounds: result misery. But something will turn up," he continued, now beaming all over his face. "I'm hopeful."

Footsteps echoed in the street and we heard banging on the door.

"Pay your debts! Open up!" called an angry voice.

"The door is locked," hissed Mrs. Micawber.

"The blossom is blighted," Mr. Micawber said, miserable again, his head in his hands. "As am I. The day sinks into unhappy night."

"I wish I could help," I said.

"You will," said Mrs. Micawber. "With your rent. Until then the cupboard is almost bare. There's hardly any supper."

We dined on stale cheese and cider, which made Mr. Micawber feel better.

"Something will certainly turn up soon," he said, waving his glass. "Let's sing a little song," and he began to warble, *"Gee up, Dobbin! Gee ho, Dobbin! Gee up, Dobbin! Gee up, and Gee Ho-o-o!"* until Mrs. Micawber declared it was time for bed.

The next day I began work in a warehouse, full of glass bottles. My job was to rinse them, hold them up to the light to check for cracks, stick labels on the full ones and cork them.

Day in, day out I worked alone, crushed with secret agony. I was ashamed of my position. I thought of Steerforth and my school friends. They had a future; I did not. I thought of my mother – gone, like a dream that ends in the cold light of dawn.

Chapter 6

Aunt Betsey

"It is time for us to say farewell," Mrs. Micawber informed me one day. "Mr. Micawber and I are leaving London."

"Where are you going?" I asked.

"To Plymouth. My family thinks Mr. Micawber will do better outside London. And I shall go with him. He is the parent of my children, father of my twins. I shall never desert Mr. Micawber."

I said goodbye to both of them and there were many tears at our parting.

"I shall never forget you," said Mrs. Micawber. "You have never been a lodger. You have been a friend."

Once the Micawbers had left, I went to begin my day at the factory. But already I had decided not to pass many more weary days there. I'd had enough. I was going to run away.

I remembered Peggotty telling me about my aunt, Miss Betsy Trotwood, who had stormed out of the house the night I was born. Perhaps she would help me.

I didn't know where Peggotty was, but I wrote to the barge house in Yarmouth in case her family knew. Back came a letter from Peggotty herself.

Dear Davy,

How wonderful to hear from my boy. I've been wondering so much where you were, and that horrible Murdstone man wouldn't tell me. Your Aunt lives somewhere in Dover. Can you get there? If not, come here. I am married to Barkis, and am very happy. Emily sends her love and so do I.

Peggotty Barkis

I had no money, though. I found a pawn shop and exchanged my jacket and hat for my fare out of London. After that I walked... for days. I was soon exhausted. My feet grew sore with blisters and my stomach ached with hunger.

One black night, huddled in a hedge, I opened my eyes in terror. A beggar shook me awake. I smelled his beery breath.

"Got any money?" he growled.

"N-no…"

"Then give me yer silk hanky. And yer shoes."

With an ugly laugh he tore them off as I wriggled away and escaped into the shadows. I was miserable, filthy, ragged and barefoot. Only the thought of finding Aunt Betsey kept me going.

At last I reached Dover. I asked everywhere for Miss Trotwood's house, and was directed to a neat little cottage. Opening the gate, I saw a lady clipping a hedge with garden shears.

"Go away," she called, waving them at me. "No beggars here."

"Please, Aunt…" I began.

"Good Lord! Who are you?"

"I'm your nephew, David Copperfield." I told her everything. When I had finished, Aunt Betsey sighed.

"I believe you. Your mother was a weak, foolish child, but she had a loving heart, and that wicked man as good as murdered her with unkindness. I should have kept an eye on her. I'll adopt you."

"Thank you," I gasped.

"That's my way of making amends. We'll visit my lawyer, Mr. Wickfield, tomorrow. I want it legally watertight, so that Murdstone can never claim you. What you need now is food, a hot bath and new clothes. I'll call you Trot," she added.

My aunt was quick and abrupt, but I felt I could trust her. I knew I'd come home.

The next day we went to Mr. Wickfield's office. A bony, pale, red-haired man showed us in.

"This is Uriah Heep, Mr. Wickfield's clerk," said my aunt. "My nephew: David Trotwood Copperfield."

Uriah extended a cold, damp hand, and I secretly wiped my hand behind my back to get rid of his clammy feel.

"I want to see Mr. Wickfield," Aunt Betsey demanded.

"Yes, madam, I'll find him, madam. I wouldn't dream of keeping you waiting. I'm humble. I know my place." He rubbed his palms together, cringingly.

"Hurry," my aunt ordered, waving her fist impatiently.

Uriah slunk off, disappearing down the corridor like a thin, white worm. "Thank you for your attention, Miss Trotwood. I've much to be thankful for," we heard him say.

My aunt explained her business to Mr. Wickfield. "I want an excellent school for him," she concluded.

Mr. Wickfield stroked his chin thoughtfully. "The best one is almost full. He'll need somewhere to board. He can live here, with my little housekeeper and myself. Here she is."

He opened a door to a room full
of books and flowers, where sunlight
sparkled through diamond panes onto
glorious oak beams and bright furniture.

By a merrily crackling fire was a girl my own age, sorting household bills.

"My daughter, Agnes," said Mr. Wickfield. "Since her mother died, she's run this house."

Agnes smiled at me. She looked so serene and sweet that afterwards, whenever I saw sunshine lighting up a room, I thought of her.

"He can start next week," my aunt announced. "Now Trot," she continued, "be a credit to yourself and to me. Never be mean, never be false, never be cruel."

Her words – and her kindness – inspired me. "I won't forget," I vowed. "I'll always do my best."

Chapter 7

Ten years later

Time, silent and gliding, creeps up on me. Once I was the new boy, then, before I knew it, I was head boy, top of the school, looking down on the line of new boys below me.

What other changes have come upon me? I wear a gold watch and chain, and a long-tailed coat. I'm training to be a lawyer, with Mr. Wickfield's friend, Mr. Spenlow. I have also started to publish magazine articles. To my delight, I am becoming well known as a writer.

And what of the little girl I saw on
my first day at Mr. Wicklow's? She is
gone. In her place, the woman I think of
as my sweet sister – Agnes, to whom I
tell everything. I confide that I am in love
with Mr. Spenlow's daughter. Her name is
Dora; she is divinely pretty, like a perfect
doll, and so tender with her little dog, Jip.

Being in love with Dora is like being in
Fairyland. I am steeped in love for her.
The sun shines Dora, and the birds sing
Dora. It is all Dora to me.

Before I knew it, I had declared my love for her and asked her to be my wife.

"I'd love to marry you," Dora sighed, blushing adorably.

"We won't be rich, I'm afraid," I said. "I'll have to work very hard."

"Don't talk like that. It's so unpleasant," she said, nestling closer, petting her dog. "Although Jip must have his lamb chop every day or he'll die."

She looked so tiny and sweet that I kissed her. As soon as it could be arranged, we married. And after the honeymoon, we came back to our new little home.

"What's for supper?" I asked hopefully the first night, after work.

Dora looked startled. "Nothing! I forgot. I was playing with Jip."

"We'll go out," I said. "It doesn't matter at all."

Night after night Dora forgot, or cooked something unrecognizable and disgusting.

We laughed about it, though I could tell she wasn't proud of herself.

"Don't scold me," she wept. "You're disappointed. I can't housekeep. I'm too silly – not like you – becoming more famous every minute with your writing."

"I love you just as you are," I said, resolving to do more than my share to help her.

Aunt Betsey saw our difficulties.

"Be patient, Trot. She's a fragile girl," she warned me.

Agnes stayed with us a lot. "Dora is so lovely," she told me. "Like a fairy princess." Agnes' sweetness made the whole house shine brighter and Dora and I both felt better for her calming presence.

Aunt Betsey was right. Dora was delicate. She fell ill before we'd been married a year and grew steadily weaker.

"I'm not going to get better," she told me faintly as I sat by her bedside. "Don't be unhappy – it's better this way. I was too young for you. I was your child-wife. You'd have grown tired of me."

"Never... Never!" I cried, holding her frail body tight in my arms.

Soon after that, my poor Dora died.

I went abroad to Switzerland, for a year, then two, living alone and writing, trying to escape from my unhappiness. From there, I wrote to Peggotty. In my sorrow, I was filled with longing to see her again.

She was overjoyed to hear from me, and begged me to come to Yarmouth, where she was living. I decided I had been alone for long enough, and set out for England, and the barge house where I had once been so happy.

Marriage suited Peggotty. Her cheeks were rounder and redder than ever.

She spoiled me with devotion, plying me with home-cooked food.

But much had changed. Emily had gone, her nephew Ham, and Daniel too.

"Emily was engaged to Ham," Peggotty told me. "He doted on her, treating her like the timid little bird she was. But a fine young gentleman came to town, and she upped and went away with him. Emily always wanted to be a fine young lady."

"What happened then?" I asked.

"Daniel went after her. We all knew that gentleman meant no good by her. He was just going to drop Emily when he tired of her – and Daniel wanted to be there when that happened, to make sure she didn't come to any harm."

Peggotty was silent for a moment, staring at the flames in the old hearth. "Ham was never the same after that. He was still as gentle as he ever was – but he'd lost all heart.

And then one day, there was a great storm at sea, and a ship, caught in the thick of it. No one else would brave the waters, but Ham dashed into the sea again and again, saving as many as he could. Then he went in one last time – right into the foaming waves – and never came out again."

"And who was he?" I asked, filled with rage at the thought of him. "This man who stole Emily from her home?"

"It was Steerforth," Peggotty said. "The friend you wrote about from school. For your sake, we made him welcome here."

"Steerforth?" I cried. In one stroke, I mourned the loss of Ham, of Emily's happiness – and my childhood hero, gone forever. I understood his true nature now. He was full of charm, but ruthless too.

I stayed with Peggotty for many months. In her loving presence, I felt my heart begin to heal. And, every day, I wrote to Agnes. She was so good to me. As I read her letters, I felt her sweet, tranquil nature calm me. Until, at last, I was ready to return to my old life once again.

As soon as I arrived, my Aunt whisked me off to Mr. Wickfield's. "There's been strange goings-on since you left," she told me. "And it must stop."

I found Mr. Wickfield much changed. His face looked haggard and his hands shook when I greeted him. Uriah Heep was always at his side, pouring him glass after glass of whisky.

"I understand what you're doing, Uriah," I said, anger clearing my mind. "You've made the old man depend on you, and alcohol, until he's lost his mind."

"Yes!" Uriah simpered. "I'm master here now. Why should I be humble all my life? I'm going to marry Agnes. She'll find she has no choice. Her father's lost his fortune – to me!"

"You fiend, Uriah!" I shouted. The thought of Agnes and Uriah together sickened me.

Suddenly I knew, as clear as light, that no one must marry Agnes, but me. I'd never forget Dora, my sweet child-wife, but I loved Agnes. I always had.

I came upon her in the bookroom, where she was reading alone by the fire. She turned her pale face to mine. "Dearest Agnes," I said, then stopped. Was it selfish to say more? But I couldn't believe she loved Uriah.

"You have always been like a sister to me. But now I long to call you something more than sister – something very different."

I saw her face glow with pleasure.

Her tears fell fast, but they were not tears of sorrow, and I felt my hope brighten in them.

"I loved Dora," I said, "but even then, my love would have been incomplete without your sympathy. And when I lost her, Agnes, I couldn't have gone on without the thought of you."

"There is just one thing I must tell you," Agnes whispered.

"What is it?" I asked.

She gently laid her hands upon my shoulders, and looked calmly up at my face. "I have loved you all my life."

I held her in my arms and felt my eyes fill with tears of pure joy.

Afterword

And now my written story ends. I remember the boy I once was, happy with my mother, then cast out and quite alone. I see the faces of my family and friends, but as I close my task these faces fade away and I see myself, with Agnes at my side, journeying along the road of life. My lamp burns low, and I have written far into the night. It is time for me to go...

Charles Dickens 1812-1870

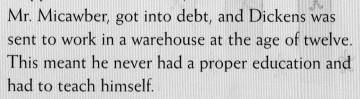

Charles Dickens, the
second of eight children,
lived in London, England,
during the reign of
Queen Victoria. Dickens'
childhood was similar to David
Copperfield's. His father, like
Mr. Micawber, got into debt, and Dickens was
sent to work in a warehouse at the age of twelve.
This meant he never had a proper education and
had to teach himself.

Dickens went on to become one of the most
famous writers of his time. His other tales include
Oliver Twist, *Great Expectations* and *A Christmas Carol*,
but he always described *David Copperfield* as, "my
favourite child."

Edited by Susanna Davidson
Designed by Michelle Lawrence
Series editor: Lesley Sims
Series designer: Russell Punter